Friend of
Mine

Faber
Stories

Thom Jones, who died in 2016, was a National Book Award finalist, O. Henry Award winner, and the author of three story collections: *The Pugilist at Rest*, *Cold Snap* and *Sonny Liston Was a Friend of Mine*. He received an MFA from the University of Iowa in 1973 and thereafter worked an array of jobs, from copywriter to janitor, until he was published for the first time, in *The New Yorker*, in his mid-forties. His stories went on to be published in other magazines such as *Harper's*, *Esquire*, *Playboy* and *Story* and were reprinted numerous times in *The Best American Short Stories*. John Updike chose his story 'I Want to Live!' for *The Best American Short Stories of the Century*. *Night Train: New and Selected Stories* was published posthumously by Faber in 2018.

Thom Jones

Sonny Liston Was a Friend of Mine

Faber Stories

ff

First published in this single edition in 2019
by Faber & Faber Limited
Bloomsbury House
74–77 Great Russell Street
London WC1B 3DA
First published in *Sonny Liston Was a Friend of Mine* in 1998

Typeset by Faber & Faber Limited
Printed and bound by CPI Group (UK) Ltd, Croydon, CR0 4YY

A CIP record for this book
is available from the British Library

ISBN 978–0–571–35197–8

MIX
Paper from
responsible sources
FSC® C020471
www.fsc.org

10 9 8 7 6 5 4 3 2 1

As soon as the turquoise blue Impala pulled in the driveway, Kid Dynamite was out of the back seat, across the lawn, into the house, and dancing out of his wool pants and tie as he vaulted up to his room. Sunday services at St. Mark's Lutheran, when communion was offered, were very long affairs. Sit down, get up, sit down again; up- and-down, down-and-up in a flesh-eating wool suit as voracious as a blanket of South American army ants. Out in the car, Cancer Frank had barely turned off the ignition switch. Kid Dynamite was already in his gray cotton sweatpants and boxing shoes. Church, man! If the boredom didn't kill you, the everlasting sermon could have you snoring in a bolt-upright position. Add to that six or seven hymns where otherwise harmless old ladies howled like they were hell-bent on shattering more than nerves – they were out to break celestial crystal. So were the small babies who screamed protest against the stagnant oxygen-deficient air and the stupefaction of body heat. What a relief to be done with it. The only reason he consented to go at all was for the sake of his grandmother, Mag.

As Kid Dynamite carefully taped his hands in his bedroom, he heard Cancer Frank's heavy wingtips scraping up the front steps. There was the snap of his stepfather's Zippo and the clatter of an ashtray being placed on the piano. In his gray sharkskin and brown felt snap-brim, with a Pall Mall draped from his lips, Cancer Frank was the Hoagy Carmichael of Aurora, Illinois. Kid Dynamite laughed to himself thinking that C.F. endured the services in nicotine withdrawal – served the chump right, too! As soon as his hands were wrapped, Kid Dynamite slipped a hooded sweatshirt over his head and was down the back stairs and out of the house. Out. Clean. Gone.

Kid Dynamite stepped through the wet grass in his boxing shoes, threw his shoulder into the side door of the garage, and stepped inside. It was cold and damp, smelling of musk. He snapped on his transistor radio. WLS was running a shitload of Sunday advertisements cheerfully promulgating the American life of living death. Kid Dynamite peered out the window where he spotted his mother, "the Driver," still sitting in the car preening in the rearview mirror. For the Driver (one trip to the Buy Right with her behind the wheel and you *would* get down on your knees and pray), church services were just another place, as all places were to her, where you went to show off your good looks and your latest outfit.

Kid Dynamite slipped on his bag gloves. It was early March and the wind was blowing hard. It had been raining off and on. Three of the garage windows were broken and the roof leaked, but the floor was made of smooth wooden planks. As Kid Dynamite did some side twists to limber up, he looked through the window again and saw his mother finally get out of the Chevy and walk into the house where there were bigger mirrors. He wondered what she had been thinking looking in that rearview. "How did I *go over* today?" No doubt.

Kid Dynamite spent a lot of time in front of a mirror himself, but only to examine his body alignment and his punching form. He was himself a good-looking young man but a realigned nose, a little scar tissue beneath the brows, and a cauliflower ear were beginning to make any comparisons with the Greek gods unlikely. Poker-faced, he threw a jab at the double-ended bolo bag and gave it a quick head slip when it bounced back. Slipping punches was the most accomplished means a boxer could employ to protect his face but also the riskiest. Kid Dynamite tattooed the bag and continued slipping punches until he began to sweat. Then he started moving in and out on the bag – started using his legs. In another few moments he was gliding around the greasy floor planks, the air so cold he could see his breath. Shadowboxing, he worked his legs, moving about the floor in a bob-and-weave style, watching himself in variously positioned mirrors. His Sunday afternoon workouts belonged to him alone and he used them to cover contingencies that had been skipped over in his regular gymnasium workouts. The old man once told him, "There are at least a thousand things that can go wrong in a fight, and how many of them can you think of –

fifty?" As with most fighters, Kid Dynamite's *things going wrong* invariably involved the problem of fear. As the old man had said, "Control your fear and you are cooking with gas, baby."

At 147 pounds, Kid Dynamite fought as a welterweight. He had recently advanced through the semifinals in the open class of the Chicago Golden Gloves, but made the finals only just barely. Two of these victories were split decisions. In his last fight on Friday, he suffered a slight cut under the left eye. The opponent had pushed him to the limit and he knew that from here on in the competition would get much rougher. Four of the boxers from the Steelworkers' Hall had made it to the finals. They were all sky-high that night, driving back to Aurora on the Eisenhower Freeway in Juan's junky-ass Cadillac. But after Juan dropped Kid Dynamite off and he came into the house with his gym bag, Cancer Frank was lying on the couch watching TV and didn't bother to even look up at his stepson. The Driver was already in bed and it was too late to call his girlfriend, Melanie. So he went upstairs and woke up the Driver. "I won. I got him good," he said.

The Driver's face was covered in a luminescent green mask. "Did you knock him out?" she said wearily. There was a bath towel on the Driver's pillow and flecks of cracked green paste dropped from her face as she spoke.

"Jesus. The creature from the Green Bog," Kid Dynamite said.

"It's a wrinkle mask. Did you knock him out or what?"

"My guy? No, I won on points. Chubby knocked his guy out. I won on points. Cuba and Eloise Greene won."

"What about your homework?" she said.

"What *about* it? It's Friday night. Man, I was feeling so right tonight. It was the best thing. I'm going to win the tournament," Kid Dynamite said.

"You're just like your father and where is *he* now? He's in the nuthouse. You've got to study. You've got geometry problems."

"I'm talking to a lima bean. Screw geometry.

6

When was the last time you had to whip out a slide rule to solve one of life's problems?"

"You hang out with those lowlife boxers and you act crude. What will you do with your life? How can you hang out with such scrums?"

"They're my friends. Jesus! I come in here feeling great. Can't you just say, 'Good, I'm glad you won. You've made me a happy lima bean.' Is that too much to ask?"

The Driver stuck her hand out groping for the alarm clock. "I've got to get up at the crack of dawn, what time is it?" she said.

"Midnight. I'm going to take an aspirin. I've got a headache. Shit!"

As he left the bedroom his mother said, "I don't want to take the wind out of your sails, but you better pass or you'll end up in the gutter."

Kid Dynamite stepped into the bathroom and closed the door. She said, "I *am* glad you won. But don't stay up all night doing push-ups; I need quiet. My nerves are shot."

He didn't bother to reply. Instead he leaned

against the sink and examined the cut under his eye in the medicine cabinet mirror. It wasn't that bad, but the tissue under his eye was swollen and tender. A couple of jabs, one good solid punch could easily burst it open. He went downstairs and got an ice cube, passing Cancer Frank on the stairs. Neither uttered a word in passing. Kid Dynamite wondered if C.F. even knew he was fighting. Suddenly the elation of reaching the finals returned to him full blown. His recent win was not merely a stay of execution. This time, one way or another, he would take it all the way. Back in bed he let the ice melt over his eye, feeling the water roll down his neck onto the pillow. He could hear Cancer Frank talking to the Driver. "He'll never get past the next round. He drew Louie Reine, the redhead that nailed him last year. It was three days soaking in Epsom salts after that —"

"Who knows," his mother said. "Maybe he's better now, he's bigger. He sure thinks he's going to win," the Driver said.

Cancer Frank said, "Not even if you tied one of

8

Reine's hands behind his back does he win."

Kid Dynamite waited in the silence of the night for this defense attorney to speak up for him. For a long time there was nothing, then came the familiar animal sounds. Christ! The two of them were having sex in spite of her stiff green wrinkle mask. Kid Dynamite rolled over on his stomach, covering his head with a pillow, but it was useless. He felt *compelled* to listen. When it was over he heard light feet squeaking on the linoleum tile, followed by intensive Listerine gargling, a hard scouring toothbrush, then footsteps back to the bed. Next Cancer Frank's heavier feet could be heard padding into the bathroom. Kid Dynamite heard his stepfather take a long horse piss and do some Listerine gargling of his own. In a moment he was back in the master bedroom where body positions were assumed, covers were adjusted, and things finally became quiet. Then he heard the Driver say, "I don't know. He was in the paper again, fifteen in a row. Knocking them out left and right."

Cancer Frank spoke matter-of-factly, without

rancor or malice. He said, "Those were prelims. Kids that don't know how to fight. This other fighter, Reine, has his number. The kid is scared. He isn't going to win. He'll blow it."

Kid Dynamite was suddenly up on the edge of the bed in a rage. He pounded his fists on the tops of his thighs. Through clenched teeth he said, "You don't know *shit*!"

Cancer Frank heard him and said, "Hey!" The voice that had so terrorized Kid Dynamite for so much of his life stabbed him now like a punch to the solar plexus. Stepfather or no, the man was supposed to guide and encourage him, not run him down and disparage his every move. Cancer Frank was the original and main source of his travail in the world thus far. Kid Dynamite imagined him poised up in bed next to his mother. C.F. said, "Watch your goddamn mouth or I'm coming in there!"

Kid Dynamite got up and crossed the hallway to the master bedroom saying, "Well, come on then, you son of a bitch. If you want some, come on!"

The Driver leaped out of bed, rushed to the door,

and locked it with a skeleton key just before he got there. "God! I knew this was going to happen."

Kid Dynamite grabbed the door handle and shook it. Then he began pounding the door with the balls of his fists. His hands were already sore from the tournament. This only intensified his rage. He threw his hip and shoulder against the door. It was an old door. Solid oak. "I'll knock down the wall," he screamed. "I'll kill that cock*suck*er!"

The Driver's voice was a vicious rasp, "You get the hell out of this house!"

In the middle of a coughing spasm, Cancer Frank choked out the words, "Call the police!"

Kid Dynamite stood at the door and listened to his stepfather cough. From the sound of it, Kid Dynamite knew he was overdramatizing. He shouted, "Go ahead, call them, you car-selling mother-fucker. I hope you *die*!"

He gave the door a last thump and went back to his bedroom where he dropped to the floor and pumped off two hundred push-ups. He knew the police would not be called. But someone would be brought in to straighten him out. Uncle Mikey, a seriously bad guy and a notorious overreactor. Since the onset of Frank's disease, Uncle Mikey had more than once dragged his nephew out of bed, kicking his ass all the way down to the basement. He came early, too, when the kid was most vulnerable. He was like some Eastern European goon squad in that regard. It would be better if the police were called – better they than Mikey.

Kid Dynamite lay awake all night in rage and anticipation. Mikey didn't show up until noon. He was wearing a suit and tie, an indication there would be no violence. At forty, the former heavyweight champion of the Seventh Army looked like he could still fight at the drop of a hat. Unlike his brother, Kid Dynamite's old man, Mikey did not become a professional fighter; he was too smart for that. Instead he went into sales and had become the most materially successful member of the family. As far back as Kid Dynamite could remember, Mikey had the best cars, houses, clothes – the best of everything. It was Mikey, however, who had introduced Cancer

Frank to his mother, and the kid's admiration for him was severely mitigated by that factor. In his suit and tie, on an early Saturday afternoon, Mikey was very solemn. Kid Dynamite knew grave matters would be discussed and threats would be issued. Compromises and concessions would be few.

After shooting the bull with C.F. and the Driver, Mikey politely invited Kid Dynamite for a drive in his new Mercedes convertible. It was a nice car and Mikey was proud of it. He talked about the virtues of German engineering as he took the river road and drove south toward Oswego. Kid Dynamite fell into a pout and nothing was said for a few miles. Then Mikey looked over at him with mounting irritation and said, "What the fuck is the matter with you? Why are you giving Frank such a hard time? He has cancer, for Chrissakes. What are you busting his balls for?"

Kid Dynamite looked straight ahead and said nothing. His body was coiled to dodge a side-arm blow, but better that than surrender his pride.

Mikey looked over and said, "I know what it is.

It's Mag – your goddamn grandmother. She's been poisoning your mind against him, hasn't she?"

Kid Dynamite kept his eyes straight ahead. "No. She doesn't poison anybody. In fact, she pays Frank's bills," he said.

"Don't get sarcastic with me!" Mikey said. "I'll pull over and give it to you right now, you stupid little fuck!"

Kid Dynamite removed the wiseass from his voice and said, "It's true. She pays."

Mikey shook his head and sighed. He removed his Italian sunglasses and threw them on the dashboard so he could rub the bridge of his nose. "Okay, I'm thinking . . . let me think. You're in over your head in this boxing tournament. 'Hard' Reine is going to fall all over you, is that it? I saw a piece about this motherfucker in the *Sun Times*. The same guy that got you last year. He ran over you like a freight train."

Kid Dynamite was sullen. "I'm better now. But how would you know? I haven't seen you at any of the fights. Personally, I'd rather be me than him. In fact, I feel *sorry* for the guy. Frank was out of line badmouthing me. It wasn't called for. That's what the whole beef is about. I don't know what they told you, but I didn't do anything except raise my voice a little."

"Raise your voice a *little*?" Mikey said. He pulled the car over to a gravel culvert where two men in bib overalls were fishing with stink bait. Kid Dynamite braced himself as Mikey switched off the engine. The big man took a deep breath and exhaled. Nephew and uncle sat watching the river for a moment. Each of the fishermen had a can of Budweiser in hand. "The beer drinker's *stance*," Mikey said. "They always stand that way. Isn't that something?"

"Nothing in there but carp and bullheads. How can you call that fun?" Kid Dynamite said. "They ought to get off their asses and do something more active. You can *buy* fucking fish."

Mikey laughed, "The problem I'm having here is that I *like* you. You act like a spoiled little brat. No harm in that. I'm trying to get past *that* so I can

15

help out. As troublemakers go, you're just a piss-ant. I was worse. Shit. There was a depression. It was different. It took the law of the fist to salvage me. Is it the same with you? I treat you decently, things are okay for a while and then you start in on him. Look," Mikey said, pointing his finger in the kid's face. "I'm on your side on this one. But you can't terrorize him in his own home. You scared the fucking shit out of him."

"I'm not a scary person," Kid Dynamite said. "I'm mild-mannered as all hell."

Mikey laughed again. He reached over and clapped his nephew on the shoulder. "Loosen up, kiddo. You're tighter than a drum."

Kid Dynamite shrugged. "I'll win the fight. I trained. I'm in shape. Once we start exchanging punches, I'll know what to do."

"Your dad had balls. He was half my size and would take on anyone. But the thing that makes you good in the ring is the very thing that makes life outside the gym impossible. I was hoping you would end up more like myself than your crazy

16

father." The glare of the sun bounced off the river, and Kid Dynamite used his hands for an eyeshade. Mikey replaced his sunglasses and said, "You're *sure* Mag hasn't been ragging on Frank?"

"Yeah, I'm sure. She knows he's sick. She doesn't rag on him. In her way, she's trying to help him."

"He's *dying*! And he's cracking up a little bit, too. I mean, why else would he be going to church three times a week? Would you like to walk in those shoes?"

"Fuckin' wingtips, not me," Kid Dynamite said. "I don't think he's going to die, either. Two packs a day. The two of them are screwing night and day —"

Mikey spoke abruptly, "You call off the dogs, okay? I don't want to hear the piss and moan."

Kid Dynamite shrugged. "They fuck like animals; it's disgusting; I got to hear it —"

Mikey raised his hand like a stop sign. "I don't want the 'wah wah, boo hoo.' Confine your violence to the ring or you're going to end up in the bughouse, like your father, a paranoid freak. The world is not that bad a place."

Kid Dynamite turned his palms up in exasperation. "I'm not a violent person. I'm a *shy* person. What do I *do*? I don't drink. I don't smoke. I *work*. I *help* around the house. You don't see my name on the arrest reports. I'm still a virgin. I don't even jack off. Fuck, I'm a super guy. The only black marks against me are that I flunked geometry three times in a row and I've got a filthy mouth. You gonna come and see the fight? I'm going to *pretend* this guy is Frank and I'm going to kick ass!"

Mikey patted his nephew on the cheek just a little too hard. He laughed and said, "All right, kiddo. In the meantime, stay out of his way for a while."

"Serious, Uncle Mikey! Are you coming to the fight?"

"I'll be at the fight. If you don't kick the guy's ass and make it worth my while, I'll be coming after you when it's over. Deal?"

"Hey! I'll kick his ass all right."

Mikey laughed at this and exchanged seats with his nephew. South of Oswego, Kid Dynamite found a straightaway and got the Mercedes up to 130 mph. It didn't seem as if the car was doing more than sixty. "German engineering," Uncle Mikey said. "Hard work, attention to detail, and a will-power that never quits." He gave his nephew a punch on the shoulder and said, "You're lucky to be a German. Who knows, someday you might conquer the world."

In spite of the cold garage, Kid Dynamite quickly broke into a full sweat. After the assault of advertisements, Dick Clark popped on the air with "Big Girls Don't Cry" by the Four Seasons and then Paul Revere and the Raiders. Kid Dynamite expected a full day of "suck" radio and he was getting it. Still, any music was better than nothing. The kid was working hard now, gliding around the floor with his hands carried high at the sides of his head and his chin tucked down. The plank floor creaked as he moved in and out on the bolo bag. It rebounded with such speed and velocity and from so many unexpected directions that he had to concentrate intently to avoid having it slap him in the face. He did flunk geometry and that was ironic. Boxing acumen involved calculating angles. The angles of the ring, Kid Dynamite understood perfectly. He would show Louis Reine angles aplenty.

Kid Dynamite had boxed him beautifully for two rounds the year before. He had fast hands and could hit Reine at will. Listening to Lolo was the mistake on that one. Reine was discouraged and out of gas after the second round. Lolo told Kid Dynamite to stay on the outside and box his opponent, "Take this one on points." So he followed the advice and boxed at long range. Then as Reine recovered his wind, Kid Dynamite got trapped on the ropes, where Reine went to work on his body. As soon as Kid Dynamite dropped his elbow to cover his liver, he got clocked along the jaw and after that it was essentially over.

This year Kid Dynamite was in shape, but he didn't actually have any better plan for Reine than before. He wasn't going to slug with him, he was going to give him angles and box. He was the superior boxer, and he was stronger than he had been the year before, if he saw a clear shot he would tee off, but he definitely wasn't going to go in trading. Although Kid Dynamite had earned a small notice on the *Beacon*'s sports page, as his Uncle Mikey had said, Louis Reine was touted in the *Chicago Sun-Times* as the premier fighter of the tournament. At eighteen, he had won forty-two fights and lost none. He had been fighting stiffer competition from the South Side and the paper said he was likely to go all the way to the Nationals.

Kid Dynamite had more fights than Reine but had suffered, in all, seventeen losses in CYO, AAU, and Golden Gloves competition. He had also got his ass kicked in a half-dozen street fights. He had been knocked cold three times, hospitalized twice. His family doctor prevailed upon his mother to make him quit after the loss in the finals the year before. But Kid Dynamite had had the fight with Reine in the very palm of his hand and he knew it. Too often, after a fighter took a single solid beating, he did not come back to the gym. Or if he did, he wasn't the same. He was gun-shy. The test of mettle was to come back with burning desire, which Kid Dynamite had done. He had not lost a fight since. He tried to explain this to his girlfriend, Melanie, the first time he saw her after the initial loss to Reine. It was a conversation that happened a year before. A tall brunette with perfect posture, she stood waiting for him at their usual rendezvous point on the corner of North Avenue and Smith Street. Melanie's ankles were squeezed together and she held her schoolbooks clutched against her breast. She was a beautiful young girl and Kid Dynamite was still something of a mess. He had a sore neck, a broken cheekbone, a black eye, and swollen purple lips. He was somewhat mystified by her tears, since his appearance had improved considerably since the fight and he had prepared her to see black and blue. Still, there were tears. He tried to reassure her. "It's not as bad as it looks," he said. "I'm just sore is all."

Light snowflakes fell on her shiny hair. Melanie had high cheekbones, a well-shaped nose to set them off, and a resolute but nice chin to better complement her heart-shaped face. She had a wide mouth and full lips, and she was quite beautiful. Her sparkling green eyes were the feature Kid Dynamite liked most. He learned to read her moods by watching her eyes. She had been the only girl he had ever cared about, and the two had been seeing one another since junior high school. Melanie was thin with frequent acne flare-ups but this bothered Kid Dynamite very little: she easily was one of the best-looking girls in the entire high school and one of the most loyal. Melanie was enough to make him believe that God was looking out for him. She approached him, reaching out to his cheek with a fuzzy woolen glove. Kid Dynamite gave her a gentle hug.

He stepped back and said, "You look so beautiful this morning. I never get tired of looking at you. It's so good to finally get out of the house and actually see you again."

"Oh, boy," she said cautiously, "are you okay? What happened?"

Kid Dynamite started to laugh but the pain of it stopped him. "He hit me so hard every tooth in my mouth rattled. But with you standing here in front of me, I'm an ace." Melanie wore a navy car coat with bone-colored toggles over her cheer-squad uniform. He said, "Why have you got the uniform on?"

"Basketball in Joliet tonight. We have a morning pep assembly. I don't want to go. I want to be with you."

They embraced again. Kid Dynamite kissed Melanie's slender neck. He could feel an erection coming on and tried to back away but she clutched him tighter. He gave in and let her hold him completely. Students were walking by, the late ones. He felt her tears rolling down his neck. "Baby, my ribs, careful!" he said.

She said, "I'm not going to the game tonight. I want to be with you."

Kid Dynamite felt hot tears of his own. He pulled his head back and kissed her. "You smell so good, you look so pretty. What you just said was the nicest thing anyone has ever said to me."

"Oh God," she said. "If it wasn't for the basketball team, I *would* have *been* there."

"You would have just seen me get creamed," he said. The procession of students hurrying to school began to thin out. Suddenly five black students came out of Fiddler's Grocery. Fid himself came out after them. He was a short heavyset man in a white apron. He stood on the wooden porch and took a final drag off his cigarette before flipping it out into the street and going back inside.

Kid Dynamite recognized the students, one of them was his friend, Eloise Greene, the club's middleweight. Jarvis Jackson packed a wet snowball and fired across Smith Street. It hit the top of the corner mailbox. Kid Dynamite tossed Jarvis the "bird" and Jarvis Jackson cried, "Hey, motherfucker! You can suck my *motherfucking* dick, man!"

Kid Dynamite dropped his books and packed a snowball of his own. He aimed it at Jackson, but the snowball didn't even make it across the street. It felt like one of his ribs had broken loose and punctured a lung. He bent over, clutching his side, as the students who had stopped to light cigarettes laughed at his pathetic toss.

Kid Dynamite looked up at Melanie and said, "I'm okay! I'm okay! Just sore and glad I missed. Jarvis a bad mo-tah scooter."

They watched the blacks proceed down Smith Street hill toward school. Kid Dynamite dried his hands by sticking them in his pockets. There was a brisk wind and he pulled his watch cap down over his ears. Both sides of North Avenue were lined with oak and maples, barren of leaves. It was a gray morning and the pristine snow was fouled by the black smoke of coal fires coming from the chimneys of the homes. Kid Dynamite stepped into a yard and snapped a small branch from a pussy willow, the first sign of spring. He traced a furry blossom around the edges of Melanie's mouth. He used his finger to trace the tears rolling down her cheeks. She wiped a wisp of tear-drenched hair from her face. She said, "My parents are at work. We can go back to my place."

Melanie's parents were both cops. Her stepfather,

Vic, had been a boxer himself, a heavyweight from New Jersey who fought in club fights as a teenager. He still followed the sport and took an interest in Kid Dynamite's career. The summer after Kid Dynamite lost in the finals of the Golden Gloves tournament, Vic drove Melanie and the Kid out past the North Aurora Downs Race Track to watch Sonny Liston train for the first Patterson fight, which was set for September in Chicago's Comiskey Park. Kid Dynamite watched Vic shell out twelve bucks to get into the old Pavilion dance hall, where a gym had been set up for Liston's camp. Kid Dynamite had never actually been inside before, but the Pavilion was the site of a number of his father's professional fights before the Second World War.

There were few spectators in the Pavilion. Vic led them to some front-row padded loge seats. The world's number one heavyweight contender was in the ring working with a very fast light heavyweight. Although his size made him seem as ponderous as a water buffalo, Liston was in fact faster than the sparring partner. He worked on cutting off the ring, something he anticipated he would have to do with Patterson, who was lightning fast and a fine boxer as well. Time and again Liston trapped the light heavyweight along the ropes. Liston threw light punches and let him go, only to trap him again. After two rounds of this, a bigger man gloved up and got into the ring. A number of handlers in gray sweatshirts with "Sonny Liston" crudely stenciled on them bustled about. One of the men simply sat before a small phonograph and played "Nighttrain," over and over again. Kid Dynamite sported two fresh black eyes incurred when his doctor had to rebreak his nose to set it right, and because of this as many people were looking at him as were watching Liston.

At the first exchange, Liston knocked his new sparring partner down with a body shot. It didn't look like much of a punch but the pain was very real. The boxer writhed about the canvas in agony. In the end he could not continue. Disgusted, and out of sparring partners, Liston climbed out of the ring and began banging the heavy bag. This went on for three timed rounds.

As the workout ran down, Liston gave a rope-skipping exhibition on the solid maple floor of the depression-era dance hall. The record player continued to blare "Nighttrain" as Kid Dynamite looked about the sparse crowd. Most of them were reporters jotting notes on press pads. Kid Dynamite heard one of the trainers tell a *Life* magazine reporter that during training Liston ate nothing but rare steak, carrot juice, goat's milk, and vegetables. He said Sonny Liston was the only private citizen in America to own a carrot juicer.

Kid Dynamite was amazed at Liston's speed and by the compactness and economy of his movements. After watching so many amateur fighters, this look at a professional heavyweight left him awestruck. Liston had a left jab that would decapitate anyone with less than a seventeen-inch neck. His display on the big bag was frightening, was light-years beyond what Kid Dynamite imagined possible. Vic gave him a nudge and said, "Bet the farm on this man. Patterson is dead."

Liston had surprisingly fast legs and was doing

double crossovers with the skip rope. Kid Dynamite looked at the fighter's feet, and when he looked back at Liston's face, he discovered Liston's baleful stare was locked in on him. Charles "Sonny" Liston was the most frightening person Kid Dynamite had ever seen, and at this moment Charles did not seem very happy. He met Liston's gaze but found it almost impossible to sustain eye contact. Soon it became an exercise in the control of fear. Sonny Liston gave Kid Dynamite the slightest hint of a smile and winked. Vic nudged Kid Dynamite again, and leaned over, whispering, "Your eyes. He's looking at your eyes."

Kid Dynamite had forgotten about his black eyes. Vic laughed and said, "I almost shit in my pants before I figured it out. That is one mean nigger."

As soon as the workout concluded, a handler tossed Sonny Liston a towel. He mopped off his face, which was glistening with Vaseline and crystal droplets of sweat. Another handler helped him into a terry-cloth robe. The towel man cut off Liston's bandages. His hands were like hams. On his way to the shower, Liston stopped just short of Kid Dynamite to sign a few autographs. He paused briefly to talk with sports writers and then looked back at Kid Dynamite. He said, "What are you, kid, a lightweight?"

Kid Dynamite jumped back as if he had been shot with a forty-five. His voice squeaked. "No sir, I'm a welterweight."

In a sissy voice, Liston said, "No sir, I'm a welterweight."

The writers roared and Kid Dynamite's cheeks flushed. Sonny Liston motioned to one of the handlers, who handed him an 8 x 10 black-and-white glossy. He said, "What's your name?"

Kid Dynamite seemed dumbstruck. Finally he said, "Make it out to Melanie."

"I thought you was going to hem and haw forever." Liston looked at Melanie. "Is that you?"

"Yes," she said.

"Looks like you thumped him pretty good," Liston said. There was another roar of laughter. A press photographer rushed over and staged a picture of Liston, Melanie, Vic, and Kid Dynamite. In the end, Liston had signed a picture for each of them. As soon as the fighter turned away and headed off to the shower, a man in a gray sweatshirt demanded two dollars each for the photographs. Vic paid gladly enough. "That was nice. He didn't have to do that."

Giddy with excitement, they compared inscriptions. Kid Dynamite's photo was signed, "To the Kid, from your friend, Sonny Liston."

Kid Dynamite beamed at the inscription like it was the writ of God. "Sonny Liston is a *friend* of mine," he said.

Kid Dynamite applied himself to boxing with renewed vigor. In the summer as he recovered from his nose surgery, he worked as a lifeguard at the city park. He would come in an hour early each day to swim. This was after he did a full morning workout in the garage. He bought a set of Joe Wielder weights. In the garage he did extra neck bridges and he lifted weights, then he ran to work and swam. For the rest of the day he rotated along the pool stations with the other lifeguards. Sitting in the hot sun in a white pith helmet, with a whistle in his mouth, he felt completely at rest.

After work Kid Dynamite would meet Melanie at the Dairybar across the field from his house. Melanie served ice cream there in a blue-striped seersucker frock. One night after closing up, they sat outside under the blue bug zapper. Melanie was an only child and although, like Kid Dynamite, she was raised by a stepfather, she did not know her own father at all.

"Maybe it's just as well," Kid Dynamite said. "Vic is really nice. My real father was nice, but he just wasn't around much. He used to take me to the gym when I was a kid. He thought I was a sissy. Took me to Chicago where I met big-time fighters. Joe Louis, Ezzard Charles, Tony Zale, Ernie Terrell – guys who were his actual friends. I don't know what I'll do when it's all over. I'm not good at anything." Kid Dynamite poked a straw in a clump of ice cream at the bottom of his milk shake.

Mikey had somehow patched up the mess with Cancer Frank. It seemed to Kid Dynamite that it was one of those rarest of occasions where he had managed to skate on something. Frank did not speak to him but neither did he criticize him. Kid Dynamite pretended that his stepfather was invisible and vice versa. Fortunately, their schedules did not converge that much. Kid Dynamite was up at four A.M. most days to run. On Monday morning he awoke with a pleasurable sense of anticipation. It would be the last run before the Reine fight. One more solid run and he would be ready. He had omitted nothing; if he lost it would be because Reine was the better fighter. On the edge of his bed, he clocked his resting pulse. Forty beats a minute.

This time around Kid Dynamite wasn't listening to any more of Juan's bullshit advice. By now he felt he knew his body better than anyone. And while he rested, the other fighters would be playing catch-up. For them it would be too little, too late. Kid Dynamite got into his sweats and combat boots in the dark. He walked quietly downstairs and out the door, falling into an easy jog across town to his grandmother's store. Since North Avenue was lit with orange tungsten streetlights, this was the route of choice; this was no time to sprain an ankle in a dark pothole.

Kid Dynamite picked up speed after the first mile. The homes along the lower part of North Avenue were three-story Victorians. Only in a few could he see the amber glow of lightbulbs. It was early, but as he passed the Burlington railroad station, he spotted commuters scouting parking spots for the trip to Chicago. As he crossed the Fox River bridge, a squad car passed and a cop waved at him. Kid Dynamite ran past the gas company and a number of factories, most of which looked like chambers of Dickensian horror. He used to like looking in the windows and seeing men at work on the graveyard shift. He had come to recognize many of them. How they could stand in front of a machine, a spot welder or a punch press, night after night was unfathomable to him. Did they suffer as he did in a high school classroom? Kid Dynamite knew that he might well end up in such a place himself. He did not deem himself college material, and he knew enough about boxing to know that his prospects as a professional were nil, just as they had been for his father. There was always someone bigger and better. Yet he was caught up into boxing and could think of little else. As he ran, the looks on the workers' faces were neutral, reflecting neither agony nor pleasure. By the time Kid Dynamite got to Lake Street he was in a residential area again. Here the houses were not so nice. He came down the hill, passed under the viaduct, and sprinted the last two blocks to his grandmother's store.

Mag was standing at the cash register going through bills. A bare sixty-watt bulb hung on a frayed wire above her. For the past few years, Kid Dynamite came in to do all of the heavy lifting for her – moving bulk cases from the basement up to the shelves. Shuffling milk and pop bottles, sacks of flour, bags of potatoes. He loaded the stove with coal and then joined Mag in the kitchen, bolting down a couple of egg sandwiches with black coffee. He opened the cupboard where Mag always had a homemade pumpkin pie. Kid Dynamite sliced a piece and shoveled it in his mouth. Mag asked him if he needed any money, and Kid Dynamite shook his head no.

The sun was coming up as he headed out, and as light flooded into the store, he saw that Mag had the "Kid Dynamite" article posted on the cash register for all her customers to see. On a shelf behind the counter she kept Kid Dynamite's boxing pendants and trophies like a miniature shrine. He waved good-bye and headed out the front door. It was a four-mile run back to the house, most of it uphill. He sprinted the entire way.

Of the four fighters the Steelworkers' Boxing Club sent to the finals, Kid Dynamite was considered the most likely to win. And as the lightest fighter from the club, he was the first to go up. He hadn't slept the night before the fight, but then he never did. As soon as Lolo taped his hands, Kid Dynamite began to shadowbox. After fifteen minutes of this, Juan forced him to sit down on a folding chair. The coach pulled a chair adjacent to him. "You know the game plan?"

Kid Dynamite nodded. He was dripping with sweat.

Juan looked at him intently. "Louie Reine had trouble making weight. Five hours in the steamroom, and three trips to the scales. Don't make your move until the end of the second round. If he's still strong then, wait until the third. Are you listening to me?"

"The old man called me. He said I should jump all over him."

Juan, normally implacable, registered disbelief, "Your old man, who's in a mental hospital two thousand miles away, told you this?"

"Yeah," Kid Dynamite said.

"Well, what do you think you should do?"

"It doesn't matter, Juan. I'm going to win tonight. I can *feel* it. I don't care what he does; I'm going to kick his motherfucking ass. I've been waiting a year to get this cocksucker."

"So you're going to do a job on him? No plan, no nothing! Just kick ass!" Juan shook his head in dismay. "Well, I hope you do. Just remember, the crowd will be with him tonight. It won't be your crowd."

Kid Dynamite got up and started twisting his neck from side to side, bouncing up and down. Lolo ducked into the locker room. He grabbed the spit bucket and water bottle. "Let's go, Kid, you're up."

Kid Dynamite entered the arena and climbed up the portable wooden steps to the ring. Louis Reine was already in the opposite corner, his red hair shorn in a buzz cut. There wasn't a drop of sweat on him. He looked the same as he had the year before. Kid Dynamite turned away, bracing his gloves against the ropes as he rubbed his shoes in the resin box. He flexed his neck and bounced up and down in his corner trying to shake off the butterflies. The referee called both fighters to the center of the ring, reminded both fighters that they had received their instructions in the dressing room, and wished them both luck.

Kid Dynamite returned to his corner, where Lolo held out his mouthpiece. He set his teeth in it, clamping down hard as he slapped himself on the forehead a few times to make sure his headgear was tight. Then he turned and looked across the ring with a blank stare as he waited for the bell. As soon as it rang, Louie Reine came rushing across the ring to engage, and Kid Dynamite did the same. Just before contact Kid Dynamite spotted his grandmother, Mag, the Driver, Mikey, and Cancer Frank seated in the third row next to Melanie and Vic. The only time in his life that Kid Dynamite could remember Mag leaving the store for more than an hour was the day she had her teeth pulled. The store was open seven days a week including Christmas Day. It had always been that way. He was so shocked to see her out of context he had to look twice to make sure he was seeing things right.

Reine gave him a Walcott stepover to switch angles, and threw a left hook that just barely grazed the top of his head. Kid Dynamite heard it whistle as he ducked under it and watched Reine's elbow sail by. He came up off balance and started a left hook of his own, aimed over Reine's right hand. Reine's punch landed first, catching Kid Dynamite high on the forehead. Because his feet were too close together, and because Reine was so strong, the force of the punch was sufficient to send Kid Dynamite reeling backward into the ropes. Reine then tagged him with a double jab and a straight right hand to the side of the jaw, and suddenly Kid Dynamite was sprawled facedown on the canvas. It seemed that the floor had flown up and hit him in the mouth. His whole body bounced hard. The canvas was as rough as concrete, and his face, elbows, and knees stung with abrasions. He had gone down like he was poleaxed, and the crowd went into a frenzy. Knockdowns, at least spectacular ones, were relatively rare in amateur boxing. The boxing reporter from the *Sun-Times,* the prophet who picked Reine to go to the Nationals, was on his feet scribbling in his notebook. It was the first thing

Kid Dynamite saw as he raised his head.

His face burned. Pinwheels spun behind his eyelids, and he shook his head hard. Looking over to his corner he saw Juan frantically motioning him to stay down and take the full eight count. Meanwhile, the referee was having a problem getting Reine to a neutral corner. Kid Dynamite distinctly saw a smile flash across Cancer Frank's face. Mag was on her feet screaming in German for him to get up. Never in his life had he heard her speak in her native tongue. Her face was red and she was pounding her cane on the floor like a savage. Kid Dynamite felt he was in a dream. Reine's corner was furiously shouting instructions, but Reine wasn't listening. His chest was puffed up and he looked supremely confident. Kid Dynamite shook his head again, trying to clear out the cobwebs. The noise of the crowd seemed very far away. He managed to get his right glove up on the lower ring rope.

Off in the seventh row Kid Dynamite focused on a big man with a fleshy bulbous nose and frosty white hair. He watched him raise his hands to his mouth and shout encouragement to Reine. For such a big man, the sound Kid Dynamite heard was diminutive, but he could hear the man's harsh South Chicago accent. Kid Dynamite wondered if his eardrum had been broken. The man continued to scream. He was well built, and wearing a plaid flannel shirt. Kid Dynamite noticed that the threads on the man's second shirt button had unraveled into tan and brown sprouts, and he thought, "Mister, take that shirt off and put it on three more times, and the button is gone." Kid Dynamite wanted to go down into the crowd and warn him. For the man to lose his button seemed like a cosmic tragedy.

The referee picked up the count from the time-keeper. He was looking in Kid Dynamite's eyes. "Five . . . six," he cried. The smile on Cancer Frank's face widened. Melanie had her face buried in her hands. Vic was on his feet shaking his fist in the air. Vic had a heavy beard and always seemed in need of a shave. Kid Dynamite was certain he could smell English Leather coming off of Vic. He could see the fine black hairs on the backs of Vic's fingers.

Next to Vic he could see the redness in Mag's face. Her skin thinned to parchment with age. She was dressed in a thick gray overcoat and pearl pop beads. Kid Dynamite had given them to her because her arthritis made ordinary clasps impossible. A six-dollar purchase. From directly behind, he heard a fan's disembodied voice say, "Don't worry, this kid is tough. He'll get up."

Time began to hurtle along again. He got up on one knee and shook his head. Goddammit if something wasn't wrong with his eardrum.

The referee cried, "Seven." Melanie lifted her head from her lap. "Eight!" the referee cried. Kid Dynamite was standing. The referee looked in his eyes and rubbed Kid Dynamite's gloves clean. "You okay?" Kid Dynamite nodded. His legs felt full of Novocain. The referee stepped back and signaled for the fight to continue.

Reine marched across the ring in a straight line. He gave the kid a real cool dip and roll, feigning a left as he fired his best punch, the straight right. Kid Dynamite anticipated this, and with the over-confident Reine walking in, he countered with a picture-perfect left hook to the point of Reine's chin. It was the best punch Kid Dynamite had ever thrown, but Reine did not go down. It was no reason for discouragement. Reine had not gone down, Kid Dynamite knew, because Reine still had hope. His job now was to erase it. He set about to do this, busily circling Reine, setting his body, and throwing punches in combination. Reine wobbled but didn't go down. The cheers of the crowd fueled Kid Dynamite's enthusiasm, but he kept his head and fought carefully. By the end of the round a frustrated Reine bulled forward, punching recklessly with both hands. Kid Dynamite returned to his corner rubbing blood out of his left eye. Juan didn't even bother with the mouthpiece, he was too busy pressing adrenaline swabs in the cut.

During the next round Kid Dynamite withstood an onslaught of sharp combinations. He methodically outboxed Reine, who began to tire and lose his composure. As Reine started throwing desperate punches, Kid Dynamite found a home for his right uppercut. By the end of the round, Reine's fair skin was marked with red welts. In the corner Juan encouraged him to go after Reine with both hands, but Kid Dynamite was exhausted as well. His lungs felt scalded by the smoke in the arena. His legs seemed as if they had never recovered from the knockdown. Juan told him Reine might have twenty seconds of gas left over after the minute's rest, to lay back and let him throw his bolt. But Reine had no gas at all. He came out arm weary and Kid Dynamite was there to pepper him with left hands. Then he moved inside, confident of his ability to slip Reine's punches. He straightened Reine with the right-hand uppercut and then threw a left-right combination, dishing out all of his mustard. It turned Reine sideways, but it did not knock him down. Reine pulled his gloves up and used his huge forearms to ward off further punishment. It was tantamount to giving up, since Reine did not mount another offensive rally. Kid Dynamite moved in and out, working his jab until the bell sounded ending the fight.

As he waited for the judges to compile their scores, Kid Dynamite chided himself for not pushing it harder when in fact he had given his all. The referee announced a split decision in Kid Dynamite's favor. Juan barely had time to pick him up and swing him around before the ring doctor jumped into Kid Dynamite's corner and pressed a gauze bandage under his eye. In the excitement of the fight, Kid Dynamite hadn't felt the cut, hadn't been bothered by it after the first round. But now the doctor shook his head, and said, "You won the fight but your tournament is over. That's a seven-stitch cut." Louis Reine came over and slapped Kid Dynamite's glove. "Good fight. I'll see you next year."

Kid Dynamite felt an overwhelming affection for Reine. "Thanks," he said. Reine, who had turned away, looked back and said, "Next time I'll get you."

The only other fighter from the Steelworkers' Hall to win that night was Eloise Greene, the club's middleweight. Greene, the cigarette smoker, caught fire and waltzed through the finals, winning the open title. For this he received a trophy, a powder blue silk jacket, and his own headline on the *Beacon*'s sports page.

Kid Dynamite did not go in with the other fighters to watch the subsequent bouts. He did not even go back to the Steelworkers' Hall to clean out his gym locker. Boxing was finally over and the real world, which had seemed so very far away all these years, was upon him.